MW00721171

A SIMPLE TASK

A SIMPLE TASK

BY MENELAOS LOUROTOS

Copyright © 2020 Menelaos Lourotos.

All rights reserved. No part of this publication may be reproduced, distributed, or transmitted in any form or by any means, including photocopying, recording, or other electronic or mechanical methods, without the prior written permission of the publisher, except in the case of brief quotations embodied in critical reviews and certain other noncommercial uses permitted by copyright law. For permission requests, write to the publisher, addressed "Attention: Permissions Coordinator," at the address below.

ISBN: 978-1-7772800-0-0 (Paperback)

ISBN: 978-1-7772800-1-7 (ebook)

Front cover image by Benjamin Mills.

First printing edition 2020.

To the family - Mom, Dad, Grandma, Grandpa, and Georgia, for your years of support and inspiration.

To Anthony, Nick, Julius, and Ben for your help in creating the film.

A Simple Task

Prologue

Now, listen here. What you are about to read is some serious shit. Apologies for the cursing, but, like everything you will read from this point on, there is a reason for uttering such a word. For one, I need a hook. Now you are hooked. For another, I am not exactly young anymore, so shame and self-consciousness are no longer in existence. Rather, the goal of not dying in regret has reached new heights, which brings us to the final reason behind my riskay opening. This is the only moment in which I curse. And why is that? You might be asking. In response, I simply say, to build trust. Trust between you and myself – you as my humble listener, and I as your frantic storyteller.

But before I frantically recite you my story, I wish to inform you that I in no way, at any point, intend for anything to come off as a lecture towards you, my humble listener. I tell you this because there is a high probability that I will, on multiple occasions, not so subtly mention and warn you about the consequences of living a life in regret. Reason being, I am currently living one. I have been a member for far longer than I care to admit. A reality that no one should ever have to face. A feeling so painful, so gut-wrenching, yet so seamless during the experience, that now, at the ripe old age of seventy-four, it is time to free myself from this intolerable state by telling you, my humble listener, a story.

This story in question is a collection of tales. Five tales to be specific. Tales which profoundly influenced the lives they themselves feature, alongside my own. Yes, they really did occur. I am not at the forefront, but one could argue that I was present and greatly affected. Why it is so important for me to be telling you these tales, I cannot say. At least, not for the time being. The same rule will apply as to why I find myself in this current position of regret. It is not easy to simply spew out what has been quietly but painfully gnawing on your heart and consuming your mind. What is important, and all I ask, is that you listen. That is all an aging fellow truly desires during their final stretch. My intention is to simply provide you, my humble listener, with a collection of tales that I feel must be exposed before my time is up. Tales that will not always reflect the tone of this opening plea. Tales that, at times, may be too revealing for my own good. Whether I will have time to tell them all, I do not know. Which is why I shall begin with the one I deem to be the most important. Just in case I happen to pass on before the collection is finally complete.

I understand that all this may sound... spontaneous. Out of the ordinary. Unclear. Even unnecessary. I agree. But at some point during every lifetime, one realizes that the unnecessary becomes the most necessary. And as someone who has always discovered his personal liberty on the blankness of an uninhabited page, you will find that everything will be revealed, in one form or another, in due time. With that, I wish to conclude with the following words: I apologize for my vagueness, my lack of explanation and specification. I apologize for my shortage of euphoria and jubilation. I apologize for my frantic nature. As I have mentioned, shame and self-consciousness are no longer in existence, but the goal of not dying in regret has reached new heights. Though, if you are currently reading, then clearly an apology is not necessary. Take what you can, as I give what I will. And all should be restored.

Sincerely,

The Storyteller

1 – Humble Beginnings

It is almost fitting that we begin with such a tale as this, Simple Task. In order to be successful, a story requires a protagonist that one must love. And by love, I do not simply refer to a romantic love, but the kind where you cannot help but adore the individual in question. The form of love where no matter what flaws that individual may possess, their ability to warm you and coddle your heart, while also, unknowingly, cracking a little smile on your face, dominates and overshadows any one of their most visible flaws. Our individual in question, our protagonist, is Alfonso.

Alfonso was a curious fellow. He was not incredibly tall in stature, in fact not tall at all. He had a tanned complexion with dark wavy hair, a little scruff on his chin, and consistently dressed on the more formal side, with his nicely ironed button-ups complimenting his faded bottoms and worn leather boots. A look that was quite respectable, yet one that would always blend into whichever setting it would enter. Always fascinated with his immediate surroundings and most comfortable with his own thoughts, Alfonso lived a life of solitude, contemplation, and routine. He would spend the vast majority of his time at the grand city gardens, which were, in the most considerate and filtered of language, a botanic spectacle of meticulous beauty. From the roses, carnations, tulips, and lilacs, to the various mosses hugging the garden rocks, to the diverse collection of cedar, maple, willow, and oak trees, all thoughtfully placed within a green space, loosely organized and guided through a web of cobblestone and gravel pathways, these gardens were something to behold for anyone, let alone Alfonso.

But Alfonso being Alfonso, would always look deeper. He would continuously consider the origins of such gardens, visualizing what he saw as a bizarre process: taking a natural piece green space, completely disfiguring it from its original state, only to recreate to our liking. A fair analysis, I must say, but one that truly defined Alfonso as a person. Although, critical of the garden's reality, it did not mean he disliked it. He would come everyday, admiring its beauty for hours on end, rain or shine. He would observe, he would draw, he would write, all while sitting beneath a young willow tree and enjoying a dash of his favourite sweet, some Turkish delight. This was the routine of someone who lived a life of triumph and adventure, and now wished to enjoy and admire the smaller things they never noticed. The routine of one who wished to live their final days in peace. Yet, our Alfonso had not even cracked thirty years of age.

It is not entirely clear what is known about Alfonso's life. What I can tell you, is that among this peaceful collection of solitude, contemplation, and routine within the city gardens, there existed a

11

reality of loneliness and a lack of purpose. At this period in time, there were no friendships in his life. There was him, his notebook and pen, and the willow tree he sat under, whom he would occasionally converse with. It is not known where he lived, or where he came from. All that was known, was that he was that guy in the gardens. Probably, because no one ever took the time to acknowledge our quiet friend, but also because our dear Alfonso, too, never made the effort. But one day, that would all change.

It was a bright and sunny day. The end of June, to be specific. The garden was at its finest and Alfonso was in his usual spot, wearing his usual attire, conducting his usual business. There was one difference, however. The typical expression of warm satisfaction and intrigue that often-flooded Alfonso's face during his daily garden visits was not in attendance. Rather, a look of concern had made its way into this lovely summer day. Alfonso sat under his friend the willow, notebook closed on his lap, gently tapping his pen against its cover. He was hesitant. Hesitant to continue with his emblematic admiration of the gardens. But why? They were arguably his second home, assuming there was a first, and anyone who had ever noticed him always linked him to the gardens he so greatly adored. Well, truth be told, within all his admirations, intrigue, illustrations, and writings, there quietly existed a powerful longing for adventure. A longing that had been suppressed beneath the desire to observe and admire. A longing that, although attractive from a distance, became intimidating when within arm's reach. At least, for someone like our dear Alfonso.

It was on this sunny June day, when our mutual friend decided to finally snatch this longing and turn it into a reality. His hesitation was the realization that the comforting days at the gardens would remain so for a definite period. Like everything else in our often-puzzling world, all good things come to an end. That is not to say that the gardens ceased to impress Alfonso, but as someone who seldom interacted with the outside world, as someone who could count the number of words he had uttered in the previous three days, and as someone who had only ever left the city for a trip to the suburbs, Alfonso knew that the time had come for his adventure.

Based off what I know, it was in this moment that Alfonso stood up, with his notebook and pen in one hand, an almost finished bottle of water in the other, and leaned against his friend the willow tree. He began to speak as if the willow was his long-time confidant, which it actually was, and stated the following words, "I can tell you where I am from, and, sadly, I can tell you where I am going," when a smile began to grow on his face, "that is, until today. Today, I am going to blur the future I know. Today, I am going to do what I have always longed to do. Today, Alfonso is going on an adventure." He took a moment to give the gardens one last appreciative gaze, the willow a farewell, and then made his departure.

13

The city gardens were within a much larger park, home to open green spaces, multiple little duck ponds, a miniature waterfall, fountains, and, like the gardens, many many trees. Alfonso had entered one of the green spaces, when he stopped to open his notebook. He flipped to the very back page, a page he had prepared for this moment, titled 'Adventure List'. There were three things under this adventure list, and being with Alfonso, they will be revealed and completed in the order in which they were written. Alfonso eyed the first of three, 'Reject the Status Quo.' An exciting start to this adventure, one would say. That is, until they read the elaboration.

Beneath 'Reject the Status Quo', indented and hyphenated, as if we were reading the notes of a university student, Alfonso's elaboration went as follows: 'litter'. Nothing more. Litter. Now, I know what you are thinking, meaning I probably do not need to echo your thoughts, but I will do so anyway because I see it as my duty to you, my humble listener, to ensure you have a complete understanding of our dear Alfonso. So yes, at first sight, what a lame and pathetic path for adventure. Litter? Really? Out of all the possibilities concerning risky, rebellious, life-changing decisions, and Alfonso elected to begin with littering. I can feel the environmentalists lurking behind me with the intention and desire of inflecting great pain towards me. To you, I simply say, go right ahead. Believe me, I am

14

definitely on your side in the grand scheme of things, but do not look at me and say that you have never suppressed the convenient urge to casually drop that candy wrapper because the previous waste bin was a block in the other direction. We have all sinned, and my criticism towards Alfonso's idea of adventure is nothing more than a deflated reaction to a hyped event. Littering is not good, yes, but let us be honest, that would not be our first idea when considering how to spark adventure in our lives. However, this is Alfonso's story. And being Alfonso's story, we shall go at Alfonso's pace.

He eyed his first quest, before shifting his focus to the water bottle he had finished while leaving the gardens. Then, while standing in the middle of the open green space, following a brief 180 check, Alfonso threw the empty water bottle to the ground and began to proudly walk away with authority. Within seconds, however, he returned with far less authority in his stride, picked up the bottle, and immediately departed in an anxious rush. It was as if he felt ashamed for what he had just done. And in all honesty, he did. Yes, he had rejected the status quo by doing the unthinkable and littering in a beautiful park, which he recognized as he made sure to tick off the first of his three adventures from his adventure list, but there was also an enormous sense of guilt for having completed the very same action. This single act tells you everything you need to know about our Alfonso, though there are bound to be many interpretations of it. Some

15

will say that he was a coward, that he did not have the courage to leave the bottle where he had dropped it, as a means to truly show his commitment to his adventure. Others will say that him retrieving the bottle demonstrated his humility, his inability to not care for his surroundings. A quality that many often wish to see in a greater number of people. As I have previously stated, I will not force my perceptions onto you. The last thing I wish to do is lecture. All that I will say, is that I believe you are both correct. Yes, Alfonso was timid. Yes, Alfonso was caring. Combined, those two traits can serve as both weakness and strength. Which side holds stronger? Well, that is an argument for another time. For now, back to our story.

Alfonso's eyes panned down to the second of his three quests for adventure. It read, 'Child play – Climb a Tree.' He smiled as he read his quest. He had never climbed a tree, but the open green area was not the place to do so, thus he made his way toward the treed portions of the park. He was not faced with the best of options, however. Remember, this is not the tallest of people we are dealing with, and nor has he ever climbed a tree. Meaning, a fully grown and aged cedar would be a bad idea. A newly planted, baby maple would just be disrespectful. These were not the only trees in the park, but it definitely seemed as if any tree Alfonso found was either too old and grand, or too young and delicate. He walked and walked, admiring the natural beauty as always, but with the pressure of completing his quest

16

engulfing the back of his mind. He began to have his version of negative thoughts, such as *maybe if I had drunk more milk, I would have more options today*. Nevertheless, he continued to quietly stroll his way to the right tree, and in due time, that right tree came along.

We will call it an adolescent tree. It was not too high or too delicate. Nor was it too grand or too young. It was just right. It stood within the edges of the treed portions of the park, just as you begin to enter the green spaces, again. It had a smooth trunk with a branch just high enough for Alfonso to reach, and strong enough to put weight on. Alfonso approached the tree until he was right beneath this branch. He looked up in excitement. "This is it," he quietly said to himself. He placed his notebook and pen onto the grass, stood up, and eyed the branch. After a few seconds, he leaped for it! He caught hold of it and held on for an astounding two seconds, before losing grip and falling to where he previously stood, his lower back landing on one of the tree's roots that had made its way to the surface. Despite this catastrophe, Alfonso immediately stood back up. He was breathing heavily, but from the shock of falling and his high levels of adrenaline. He looked around to see if anyone had witnessed his shenanigans and up to see if he had damaged the tree in any way. Not a leaf in flight and not a person in sight. A small part of him was disappointed that he had not caused a scene, but he continued, nonetheless.

His second attempt clocked in at three seconds, his third at four, and his fourth at one. At this point, he was a moment away from giving up. Amidst his breathing, this time from exhaustion and frustration, he uttered, "one more time." Regaining his composure, he took a few steps back in preparation for a run up. He eyed the branch as if he was a predator and the branch his prey, and darted towards the tree. He made his final jump, the moment he stood just prior to beneath the branch. He caught hold of the branch, but this time used all additional strength and momentum to swing himself into position to hug the tree trunk with his legs. In the blink of an eye, Alfonso found himself in the most secure of positions, with his back facing the ground and his eyes looking directly into the tree's canopy. He swiveled his head to view both realities, before taking a moment to appreciate his accomplishment. He had done it. He had committed an act of child play. He climbed a tree.

Within seconds of admiring his accomplishment, Alfonso made his way back to ground level, did a brief celebration (the kind a hockey player would do after scoring a goal), and continued his adventure. He ticked off the second of his three quests, before running his pen over the third and final one. The one that, unlike the previous two, would actually challenge Alfonso, pushing his comfort levels to their outer rim, and serving as the single most profound change his life had ever encountered. The third and final quest read as follows: 'Talk to a Stranger – Make a Friend.'

We know Alfonso was lonely. It did not help him that he spent his days at the city gardens, while most people were working. A slight issue for his adventure as well. He chose to wander through the park's open spaces, in hope that he would find someone playing with their dog or enjoying a midday picnic. Of course, being a late weekday morning, the park presented a rather desolate reality. It was too early for the lunch break crowd to occupy the benches along the pathways, and too late to run into any of the seniors on their daily morning walks. All kids were in school, meaning no families were in sight. It was just Alfonso. Strolling through the park's green spaces, he headed back for the forested regions. He eventually returned to the tree he so heroically climbed, marking the part of the park where the open green spaces met with the treed portions, as mentioned. Alfonso referred to this area as the borderlands.

He entered the park's forest and wandered through its walkways, some gravel paths and some wooden boardwalks. He even pondered the notion of taking a break to sit back and admire the trees, but fate would have other ideas. He almost succumbed to his desires, until he heard a voice in the distance. Now, apart from being the first voice he had heard all day, there was something unique about this particular one. It was not the sound of casual banter. Nor was it

19

reminiscent of an adversarial discussion. There was a certain allure to its tone. A sense of grandness and importance to its echo through the trees. There could not have been a more obvious sign – follow the voice!

The mysterious voice dragged Alfonso through undiscovered sections of the park. He took paths he had never seen, to the point where these paths ended, forcing him to do the unthinkable and continue off them. As anyone would predict, he hesitated before making a decision. The idea of venturing into these untampered areas bothered him. The lack pathways was due to the steep terrain, and Alfonso had heard the rumours of wolves nesting, coupled with the occasional sighting of skunks and racoons. A collection of troublesome and frightful obstacles, for our dear friend. But with the echo of the mysterious voice growing in size and in enticement, he had no other choice but to pursue it. Not only was his curiosity entranced by it, but his adventure depended on it.

As he carefully made his way through this unchartered territory, he was pleasantly relieved not to have encountered any of the rumoured critters. The only confrontation was with an owl that was half asleep, which was more of a treat than a scare. He made note of where he met his new acquaintance, to potentially plan a visit after his adventure was complete. The intriguing voice ceased partway through his search, only to restart minutes after its recess, and then fade off once again. "Where could they be? Who could they be?" Alfonso muttered under his breath as he marched through the bushes of the unknown. The silence made him uncomfortable. The thought that he may discover nothing stressed him. *How would I get back?* he thought. And to make matters that much more irksome, a new obstacle had arisen... A call of nature, to put it lightly. Having to pee badly, to put it bluntly.

Frustration swarmed Alfonso. Not only had he lost track of the mysterious voice, but he had a sudden and violent urge to urinate in the unknown center of the grand city park. Never mind the fact that he considered any form of public urination to be taboo, no matter what the circumstance. The notion of committing such an act was beyond belief, but the second notion of accidentally damping his pants while on adventure was terrifying. He looked around to ensure there were no witnesses, though who would be where he was to begin with. He then apologized to the shrubs and conducted his business. As he finished, he heard a rustling from the bushes behind him. He did not want to turn around. The idea and reality frightened him, but he would have been foolish not to do so. So, he did. His heart was throbbing and his stomach was sobbing. There was anxious pain throughout his body. *Could this be the end of the adventure? That would be a shame.* He turned to see what he least expected... A pigeon. "Oh?" he blurted in surprise, "I didn't expect to see you," he added with a dash of

21

relieved joy. "How could someone as small as you make so much noise?" The pigeon turned around for a few moments and then rotated back to face Alfonso. Alfonso was puzzled. The pigeon repeated. Alfonso, still confused, decided to look in the direction the pigeon repeatedly turned to. It was a decision that reignited anxiety throughout his body. He stood still, stiff as a bureaucrat and growing paler by the second, as his brown eyes met the deep blue eyes of a wolf standing within the bushes. The notion of dampening his trousers no longer seemed socially unacceptable.

The two sides stood facing each other, while the pigeon wandered in circles between them. The only sound that one could hear was that of the gentle wind making its way through the trees. After roughly a minute, the wolf began making slow strides towards Alfonso. Alfonso remained still, attempting to gather his thoughts and formulate a plan. A plan was formulated. He would hope that the wolf would walk by, maybe casually greet him with a sniff, before disappearing into another set of bushes. *Yes. This is the best plan.* As far as he was concerned, running was hopeless. The wolf was made for that kind of skirmish, meanwhile Alfonso had not run since he was falsely accused of shoplifting in the ninth grade. Throwing a rock or branch at the wolf would only spark a chase, and attempting to offer it the pigeon in exchange seemed unfair and unlikely. All he could do was hope. He continued to stand still as the wolf approached him.

There was still distance between them, but a small enough amount that the calm approach could transition into a bolt at any second. I guess the wolf was not phased by Alfonso, considering they often hunted in packs. But to be fair, who would fear our protagonist?

As the gap narrowed, Alfonso began to close his eyes. He could hear the rustling of the bushes. *This is it*, he thought in conclusion, and simply prayed that something would prevent this unfortunate ending to his adventure. It appeared that his prayer was indeed heard, for at that instant, a voice erupted from a short way's away. Alfonso's eyes popped open and he quickly spun around to see if there was someone behind him. No one stood there, but the voice was coming from not too far away, and was quite familiar. "The voice!" Alfonso exclaimed in a loud whisper. He turned back around to look out for the wolf. It had vanished. The pigeon remained, waddling about, before it took flight and headed in the direction of the voice. "Fair enough," Alfonso said. He browsed the area to confirm that the Wolf was truly gone. He saw nothing and cracked a little smile. He opened his notebook to the 'Adventure List' and wrote 'Defeat a wolf' with a tick next to it. He closed it and followed the voice, yet again.

2 – A Simple Task

If there has ever been a time when the expression 'light at the end of the tunnel' has been the most applicable, it was during these very moments of Alfonso's adventure. As he neared the origin of this mysterious voice, new layers of sunlight appeared. The density of the trees began to diminish, as Alfonso noticed the remnants of what appeared to be old caution tape and construction fencing. The thinning of the trees featured a growing number of stumps. It appeared as if there had been an effort to remodel this section of the park. Alfonso was intrigued, but this was the last of his concerns in the given moment.

The more the light opened itself to Alfonso, the more of the voice Alfonso heard. That is, until it came to an abrupt stop. Alfonso matched his cabalistic opponent. He waited for a few moments to see if the voice would return. Nothing. "I don't understand," he said to himself. A dash of anxiety made its way into his chest. "This better not be the que for the Wolf." It was in this moment when he noticed some movement up ahead. No, it was not an animal, but what appeared to be a person. A fierce war of emotion erupted within him. Excitement challenged fear for the throne, as Alfonso, carefully but excitedly, made his way towards the mysterious figure. He hid behind each tree he approached, to ensure that no premature, public introductions would occur. Eventually, there were no more trees to hide behind, as any step further would enter a clear-cut circular patch of surprisingly level ground, with a single tree stump remaining in its center. On this stump, stood a tall, lean gentleman, dressed in casually formal attire (the outfit of a travelling salesman), while holding a leather briefcase. Alfonso, from behind that final tree, looked on in intrigue. *Who would stand here alone?* he thought, *what on earth could he be saying?* And sure enough, Alfonso's questions would be answered.

"Hear ye! Hear ye! Please step forward, drop your emotional barriers, eradicate any concerns you may have about my state of being, and come forward to partake in the listening, and the later accepting, of an unbelievably enticing proposal! I, The Working Man, am here for you." It was like something out of Shakespeare. And by that, I do not make reference to any specific Shakespearean tale or hero, but rather to the theatrical reality. The Working Man was the star at the Globe and Alfonso his fortunate spectator. At least from the supposed perspective of The Working Man, who had not yet even noticed Alfonso.

For Alfonso, only one word embodied his thoughts towards what he was witnessing: befuddlement. He was not afraid, but nor was he particularly happy, which did not mean that he was unhappy, but definitely meant that he was not unhappy or afraid. Intrigue could be found in his basket of emotions, but for the most part the selection was dominated by suspicion and complete utter confusion. Alfonso asked himself again, "Who would stand here alone? Who is he talking to?" as The Working Man continued to patiently stand upon his stump, maintaining the largest of smiles, not knowing his voice had been heard. The whole situation felt all too surreal for Alfonso. He decided to test this reality and pinched his left arm. The feeling was minimal, which concerned him before he realized his arm was numb from leaning against the tree for so long. As this initial concern faded, he proceeded to his right. He wished to make this pinch count, for the sake of reassurance.

After carefully feeling his right arm and locating a sensitive spot over his tricep, Alfonso unloaded, what was later referred to as, 'The Pinch'. The notion of a dream crumbled quickly as his nail dug deep into his skin. The pain was one that we have all experienced – sharp, but short, but sharp. It sparked a gasp, a slight loss of balance, and the crunching of a small twig that lay near the trunk of the tree he hid behind. Physically, Alfonso was fine. Unscathed, apart from his newly born pinch mark. Yes, the short but sharp pain caught him off guard, but the crunching of the small twig overshadowed the pain and its shock. Its demise frightened Alfonso. The moment he stepped on that twig, he slowly and anxiously lifted his head to meet the uncontrollably elated face of The Working Man. No words could describe or illustrate this purest of happiness that gleamed from within The Working Man. At least, no words apart from his own. "You sir! Come forward!" he excitedly demanded of Alfonso.

"Who? Me?" Alfonso replied in a panic. He knew that he responded with pointless words, but what else would he have done? Run?

"You sir! You have clearly the sound of my voice! You must have persevered in order to find it, and eventually me, and now I am beholden unto thee. And in return, I must present to you the grandest of offers. One, that if accepted, will drastically improve your living experience. So please, in good faith, come forward." The words were perfect given the context. The Working Man lived up to his Globe-like presentation. No one would deny this, including our anxious Alfonso. Never in his wildest dreams did he expect any of this to happen to him. It was strange, surreal, uncomfortable, but most importantly, exciting. He accepted The Working Man's request and approached him. "You seem hesitant?" The Working Man pointed out as Alfonso walked carefully towards him.

"Well… as one should be in this position. No?"

"Nonsense! This is a position of fate. Of trust, if you will, between you and me, and this environment in which we share," replied The Working Man as he gestured towards the park forest and the open,

27

circular patch of grass that he and Alfonso currently occupied. "I have stood in this wretched place for three days! Waiting for the potential of life and someone to take me seriously! Three have come. One, ran away at first sight. One, verbally abused me, profusely, for several hours! And one stayed. You! You are the one who stayed! Now tell me, doesn't that feel special?" Well, it did. Alfonso could not deny it.

"You got me there," Alfonso agreed as he released a small smile.

"You see? Fate! There is a reason behind you being the one that stayed. There is purpose to this encounter. That, I can promise you." Alfonso's eyes widened at the sound of 'purpose'.

"Are you sure that's a promise you can keep?" he asked of The Working Man.

"Like I said, I have stood in this wretched place for three days! Three days! Waiting, for the one who would stay. For the one who would accept my enticing proposal. My friend, there is purpose within us and purpose between us. I cannot speak for you, but I will speak for myself." What followed was the uttering of the most important words Alfonso had heard in a long time. Words that would influence him far beyond this little story. "My purpose, is to deliver purpose, as a means to achieve my purpose." Alfonso pondered these words as The Working Man continued, "My enticing offer is as follows," The Working Man reached behind the stump and retrieved a leather briefcase, "deliver this case to the following address, and you will handsomely rewarded." He handed the briefcase and a small piece of paper with an address to Alfonso.

"That's it?" Alfonso asked with suspicion.

"That's it," replied The Working Man. "A simple task, for a handsome reward," he concluded with a smile and a wink.

"What do I do after I delivery the case?"

"That is for you to discover."

"And the reward?"

"That will be presented in due time. For now, deliver the case."

"What's in the case?"

"That I cannot tell you. And nor should you look! Otherwise, your reward will be in jeopardy. Also, on your way you will be joined by a fellow compatriot – The Scribe. They will accompany you on your journey."

"And how will I know 'The Scribe' when they arrive?

"Trust me, you will." Alfonso found himself in a peculiar state of emotions. As throughout his adventure, they were mixed. It would not take a genius to tell you that this whole exchange, this whole interaction, and reality, contained the biggest and boldest of red flags. Even the most trusting of people would find The Working Man and his enticing proposal to live on the sketchy side of the street. Alfonso knew this and felt it all too well. On any other day, he would have fled

29

the moment he snapped that twig. But today was a different day. Today, he had ambitions. He took one look at the briefcase and a second one at his notebook before facing The Working Man, who continued to maintain his joyful expressions.

"Okay then. Let's hope fate continues to be a positive force," Alfonso stated as he released a small exhale.

"I can only expect it to do so, Mr…"

"Alfonso. Just Alfonso."

"Alfonso!" The Working Man announced in his Shakespearean tone, "Best of luck."

3 – The Journey

It was safe to say that Alfonso left his newly made acquaintance with a new assortment of emotions. The mixed anxieties and curiosities that had accompanied him to his meeting of The Working Man were still alive and well, but were now partially numbed by newly adopted skepticism and shock. Skepticism towards the 'enticing proposal' he had accepted, and shock towards the fact that he had actually accepted this 'enticing proposal'. He had no clue where he was going, and no clue who or what he would encounter.

He left The Working Man's place of… operation and followed the path he had previously taken to reach it. The thought of encountering the wolf concerned him, but luckily the only contact he made was with the owl. He briefly paused to admire and acknowledge it with a smile, before continuing on.

Two hours felt like minutes as our Alfonso exited the park, walked through town, and found himself strolling within the quiet side roads of a quaint neighbourhood. The streets were clean and lined with trees. The grass between the sidewalk and the road was lush and neatly trimmed. The homes ranged in shapes, sizes, and colours. They all appeared as if they had a fresh coat of paint tossed on no more than a couple days ago. If a neatly trimmed and lush lawn was not in play, a small garden of flowers, vegetables, and the occasional fruit tree made up for its absence. The streets themselves were silent, as it was midday and school was still in session, with only the occasional bird and a soft breeze whistling its way through the trees and gardens, providing gentle sounds to fill the day.

Alfonso appreciated these new surroundings, for reasons we can already guess, but his uneasiness towards the 'simple task' clouded his appreciation. He stopped walking, took a look at his surroundings and then the briefcase. "What am I doing?" he said to himself.

"That is a genuinely important question. And if I may say so, don't let your guard down." Alfonso swung around in a panic. Behind him, by roughly ten feet or so, stood a lanky, bearded man, sporting a worn wool suit, brown in colour excluding the white button-up, suspenders that were just visible beneath his blazer and vest, a flat cap, and a pair of beat up black dress shoes, while carrying a leather-bound journal and a fountain pen. To anyone else, the first assumption would be that they ran into some hipster. And if we are honest, Alfonso dabbled with those thoughts as well. However, considering his situation, the man's pale complexion and baggy eyes, Alfonso leaned upon his natural inquisition.

"Let me guess, The Scribe?" he asked. The man smiled.

"Let me guess, Alfonso?"

"I'm not even going to ask how you got here."

"That would be a pointless question, yes." There was a brief moment of silence. The Scribe maintained his smiles, as Alfonso continued to stand in hesitation.

"You followed me?"

"I followed you." A second silence ensued, with both men maintaining their positions.

"Serious question," Alfonso stated.

"Serious question it is."

"What am I doing, exactly?"

"A great opening!" The Scribe exclaimed.

"Excuse me?" The Scribe opened his leather-bound journal, uncapped his pen, and began to write.

"What am I doing, exactly? Alfonso pondered," he said while writing. Alfonso had no response. He remained standing, looking on at what he was witnessing. He did not know whether to be confused or irritated, concerned or excited, or even the entire mix. The Scribe looked up to face him after pausing his writing, only to continue moments later. "He displayed hints of frustration and perplexity as I continued to ignore his question in order to describe his expressions." Not knowing how to respond, Alfonso elected to walk away. He frankly did not have the patience for these games. "You're doing the right thing." Alfonso stopped in his tracks and turned to face The Scribe, who had not budged nor lost his enthusiasm. Alfonso maintained his disgruntlement.

"How so?" he responded.

"What did you do this time yesterday?"

"Walked through the city gardens."

"And the day before?"

"Also walked though the city gardens." The Scribe shrugged and smiled.

"Need I say more?" This response sparked a surprising chuckle from Alfonso.

"You haven't exactly said enough." The Scribe then added a chuckle of his own.

"It isn't my job to do so."

"A true scribe, then."

"A true scribe. I accompany. I observe. I record. Those are my duties."

"And what purpose do they and you serve?" Alfonso asked with slight authority.

"To serve your purpose!" The Scribe happily replied.

"Of completing this simple task…"

"Precisely! Don't allow your skepticism to disrupt your task at hand. You willingly stumbled upon this… simple task. And now, you must carry it out. Believe me, you are doing the right thing. As surreal as this all may appear to be."

"May appear?"

"Do not doubt. Do not forget. Simply do." Alfonso would have been a child if he had convinced himself that The Scribe's words left no effect on him. In what had become a custom on this journey of his, he glanced over at his notebook and then the briefcase. It was one of his longer glances that, coupled with the words of The Scribe, may have injected some extra belief into his journey.

"Okay," he said.

"Good! I knew you were the right choice from the moment I saw you." Alfonso cracked his first genuine smile in a while. A warm feeling grew within him. "Now if I were you, I would make it to that address as soon as possible," The Scribe spontaneously added. The warm feeling and smile quickly vanished.

"Why?" asked an anxious Alfonso. The Scribe turned to his journal and began to write.

"Alfonso displayed grave concern upon receiving warning about the imminent danger he would potentially face."

Never in his life had Alfonso run so quickly. Within five minutes, he had anxiously made his way to the address he was given

35

by The Working Man. The Scribe calmly followed along, as a frantic Alfonso run was not the most challenging of paces to follow. He arrived only a couple minutes after our protagonist, finding him regaining his breath outside his final destination. "This is it," Alfonso said to The Scribe the moment he saw him. They stood outside of a white home sitting on a corner lot, outlined by a traditional picket fence. They were by the front gate, facing the home's front lawn and its collection of bushes and flowers along the fence.

"I know," The Scribe assured him in his usual joyful tone. Alfonso gently shook his head.

"Right. Okay, let's go."

"Not just yet."

"What?"

"Not just yet," The Scribe repeated with a smile, this time looking down and writing in his journal. Alfonso stared at him.

"And why?"

"We must wait."

"For what?"

"For who."

"For who?"

"Yes, for who."

"Alright. For who?"

"For whoever wishes to enter our world." Alfonso surprised The Scribe with a laugh.

"And why would anyone care?" The Scribe stopped writing and faced Alfonso.

"Because it could be a story worth telling."

"Following someone transporting a case from park to cookie-cutter house, as a story worth telling?"

"That someone is you. The protagonist of this... simple task. A protagonist walking into the unknown. Always an exciting endeavor!"

"An unknown that was just said to contain potential danger."

"Correct." Alfonso gestured towards The Scribe.

"Yet, the messenger –

"I prefer orator."

"The orator... continues to happily promote this 'simple task' as exciting adventure."

"Also correct. And if I may, you never struck me as the chatty type," The Scribe added with a wink. He was not wrong, of course.

"Things can change when in danger," Alfonso responded in a slightly more defeated tone. Yet, The Scribe took a turn at laughter.

"Who said you would be in danger?" Alfonso was stunned. Almost lost for words.

"Do I really need to answer?"

"People typically do when asked a question."

"When asked a genuine question."

"What makes mine ingenuine?"

"The fact that you told me I would face danger if I didn't rush over to this address."

"I never said that."

"Please don't play that game with me."

"I'm not playing any game apart from our game of life. I said potential danger. I never warned of certain danger because the certainty wasn't a reality." The Scribe then lowered his head to resume writing. Alfonso looked on in amazement. *What did I get myself into?* His initial anxieties met frustration. In a bizarre fashion, arriving at his final destination brought more confusion than clarity. He stood just feet away from the entrance to what could conclude this 'simple task', but was held back by the flimsy yet effective persuasiveness of The Scribe, who continued to write only God knows what. But Alfonso wanted answers, he wanted reassurances, and going against his Alfonsonian tendencies, he pushed on.

"All I ask is for some honest clarity. No fuzziness. No games. Just pure clarity." The Scribe chuckled again. He continued writing for a few moments more, as Alfonso waited impatiently. He then raised his head, maintaining his smile as always, and spoke. "The Caretaker."

"The Caretaker?"

"The Caretaker. The one who will have interest in your journey."

"I see… And this is their home?"

"Some would say that."

"Some would? Who would not?"

"Others." Alfonso let out an extended exhale.

"This is ridiculous. Enough with your games." Alfonso went to unlock the front gate. As he reached over to flick the lock, an arrow struck the gate's wooden paneling. He froze and slowly raised his head, until an unfamiliar voice made its entry.

"You don't look this way until I say so," said a bold, grizzled, masculine voice. Alfonso held his frozen position. All he could hear were the sounds of The Scribe's writing, the footsteps of the person who had spoken making their way towards him, and the gentle sounds of the natural world playing about these unprecedented events. All he could see, was the paved pathway that led to the front door of the house, the lawn which hugged the pathway, and the small collection of flowers growing close to the fence.

The sound of the footsteps continued to grow with every passing second. Alfonso remained still, sweating from both anxiety and his acrobatic position, but paid close attention to the footsteps and their tone. Whoever this was, they were no athlete but not necessarily out of shape. The steps were heavy as they hit the ground, but approached Alfonso at an above average pace. That pace came to an end the moment the footsteps entered Alfonso's view. They stood in silence as Alfonso stared at a pair of, what he believed to be, Tasmanian Blundstones in the most worn possible state. All that was left to hear was The Scribe's endless writing. It was as if mother nature herself paused to witness this moment. "You can face your obstacle and press on, or quietly turn and leave for good. The choice is yours."

4 – The Obstacle

As with many encounters, dilemmas, predicaments in our lives, the choices we must make are both clear and painful. We know what is right and wrong, even if we are afraid to admit it. A reality well known to our Alfonso prior to this… simple task. But of course, as everyone says, firing arrows is not safe. Another reality understood by our Alfonso. He knew what was right and he knew it would be painful, slowly rising to face his new adversary. In addition to the worn Tasmanians, the elusive fellow wore a pair of black jeans, a poncho straight out of a spaghetti western, which sparked major assumptions about potential headwear until his hatless, balding head was revealed. The man himself was average in height, slim in build, though not as slim as The Scribe, and slightly unshaven. He stood eyeing Alfonso, holding a crossbow. Alfonso also elected for eyeing his new adversary, as there was not much else to choose from. Especially, with a weapon in the mix. The two stood in silence for roughly thirty seconds. "Greetings," the man then said, maintaining his emotionless position.

"Hello," responded a cautious Alfonso.

"Hello to you too," responded the man. Silence again. Apart from The Scribe and his business, that is. Neither Alfonso or the man broke their stares, the man's cold and lifeless, and Alfonso's inquisitive and baffled, each defining their current position. Alfonso was the first to break contact, quickly scanning the man's intriguing outfit before returning to face him. Again, the man did not flinch, but as it intimidating as the context of this position was, it was just as simple to reveal its comedy – that being the man and his outfit. Our protagonist had seen a lot, thus far. A lot of what anyone would describe as outrageous, surreal, ludicrous, or unbelievable. *I've seen it all*. A thought he always dreamed to consider. He smiled, lost in his mindfulness. "Oh, you find me amusing?" the man abruptly interjected.

"No no," Alfonso assured in fright, as he snapped out of his thoughts. "Not at all."

"Not at all?"

"Not at all."

"There is nothing amusing about me?"

"Not that I can see," Alfonso lied.

"Nothing out of the ordinary? Nothing that would cement this image in your mind?"

"No. You're as normal as one can be," said Alfonso, attempting not to glance over the man's outfit yet again.

"Normal," the man stated.

"Yes."

42

"Not extraordinary."

"Yes," Alfonso said, this time with hesitation.

"Lacking the memorable effect?" The man's expression had yet to change. Alfonso thought carefully about his response. He chose to nod. "Let's summarize then," began the man, "You arrive at a home... Is that fair to say?"

"Sure."

"Sure?" questioned the man, "You're not certain?"

"Well..." Alfonso began.

"Well what?" interrupted the man almost instantly, "Is this not a home?" he asked, gesturing towards the white house. Alfonso looked at the house and then lowered his eyes, pondering his response. His eyes once again met his dear notebook. "I can't call it a home," he said, his eyes still lowered. Silence. Even from The Scribe. Alfonso waited for a potential response, a potential sound, but nothing felt his hope. He looked up. There was a slight change in the man's expression. A small, but noticeably inquisitive gaze.

"Why is that?"

"Home is a powerful word. A personal one. It's where you live and sleep, eat and drink, read and write, watch and listen, think and dream. It's the one place that is a constant in your life. The whole world can change around you, but your home will always be your home. It will always be there for you. Unless, of course, you decide otherwise, but I doubt anyone would give up on something so personal. So special. That's a home. This is a house," Alfonso concluded by pointing to the white house. It was only then when he realized his little speech had somewhat consumed him. It was one of those instances when you are so invested in what you are saying that for brief moments afterwards you do not recall what exactly you said or did. Alfonso had in fact made no eye contact with the man during his spiel. His eyes focused on the house in question, his final destination, the one place that would finally reveal to him the purpose of this… simple task. Their refocusing revealed an unexpected turn of events. The man with crossbow stood smirking with a half smile.

"One lesson that no person is capable of learning is, to always expect the unexpected," he said. "I did not expect those sort words to come out of this sort of person," he added, pointing towards Alfonso. Alfonso released a smile of his own, hoping to ease the earlier tensions. He turned around to see if The Scribe had left, only to find him standing, smiling, and giving a thumbs up before returning to his writing. Alfonso let out a smirk of his own. *Progress*. He turned to face the man at the gate, when he came across a shocking sight. The man had not moved, but in addition to his crossbow he held a new arrow. His smile had grown as Alfonso's passed on. "Allow me to demonstrate," he began, "when you know that the truth is not being told, the first thing you do is reload." He armed the weapon. Alfonso froze. A wave of emotion erupted within his gut. "Then," the man continued, "you approach the source of these lies and aim." He took two steps towards Alfonso, literally standing close enough to feel any breathing, placed the weapon against Alfonso's chest, and looked him straight in the eye. "What I'm holding against your chest is a symbol of medieval times," he uttered with a menacing whisper. "Times that hosted enormous violence. Some would call them barbaric. All would call them dangerous, with this little guy here serving as a reminder, built to puncture the strongest of armor never mind your flannel. Which leads me to ask the following familiar question: Do you feel lucky?" Alfonso stood still as could be. To say he was scared would have been an understatement. His clammy hands, damp undershirt, and explosive heartbeat spoke for themselves. His breathing was intensive but not fast. It was obvious to the man that Alfonso was trying to control his breathing, rather than charge into a panic. "Well, do you, punk?" he added for good measure.

"No."

"Understandably so. Tell me, what's on your mind in the midst of all this?" The truth is, there were two things on Alfonso's mind during this moment. The first regarding The Scribe's calmness throughout the entire exchange. He had continued to write without pause. *The bastard!* Alfonso thought. The second thought, however, was of greater importance to him. One that he was afraid to ask, but desperately needed to know.

"If I say," Alfonso began, "will you guarantee my safety?"

"Ha! No one can guarantee anyone's safety," replied the man as he added more pressure to Alfonso's chest. "So, I recommend you spit it out." Alfonso simply sighed.

"Is it always this quiet around here?" he finally asked. The man maintained his threatening gaze for a few moments more, when it suddenly gave way to enormous laughter. He withdrew the crossbow and placed it back to his side, as he slowly regained his composure. Alfonso, as he had frequently done throughout this journey, looked on in confusion. When the man finally gathered himself, he relaxed his posture and faced Alfonso. "I like you," he said with a smile - the first that Alfonso had seen. The man then turned to The Scribe. "You finally bring someone worthwhile!" The Scribe, as always, completed his writing before responding.

"Hate to agree with you, but yes. We found our guy," The Scribe responded with a tiny chuckle. Alfonso watched suspiciously. Although relieved that the crossbow had departed, he knew better than to assume that things were normal. "Does this mean I can pass through?" he asked.

46

"Ha!" the man laughed again, "Of course not. You still haven't explained why you tried to break into this lovely home."

"Break in?" Alfonso replied in surprise. This response had legitimately taken him aback.

"You seem surprised."

"Well yeah. Apparently, I'm your guy."

"That doesn't change the fact that you tried to break into a home."

"Those are an extreme choice of words."

"How would you describe it then?"

"Opening a gate to go knock on a door…"

"And did the person in residence know you were coming?"

"Given my situation, they might have."

"In other words, no."

"That's not what I said."

"You didn't have to say it."

"Because I didn't."

"There's no fooling me, kid. I have been around long enough to have seen most things. And as the caretaker of this home, your actions are of both great concern and interest to me. So tell me, why are you here?"

"You know why I'm here."

"Perfect! Then it shouldn't be an issue to say." Alfonso rolled his eyes and sighed as he responded.

"I'm here to deliver this case."

"No you're not."

"I'm not?

"Nope. Try again." Alfonso stood silently.

"I am doing a favour for The Working Man," he answered with hints of doubt, as if he was being tested.

"Oh dear, oh dear, that was even worse!" The Caretaker announced before ending off with a sigh. "Maybe I spoke too soon about you."

"I'm sorry, but… I have to admit, I'm confused."

"Evidently. Well, you leave me no choice. And I am only doing this because I do actually like you. I want you to know that. So, here we go. I'm going to fill you in on a little secret… Alfonso?"

"Yes."

"Alfonso," The Caretaker confidently confirmed, "you are on an adventure!"

"Yes, yes, so I have been told," Alfonso replied with irritation.

"No no," The Caretaker began as if he were lecturing a child, "it's more than someone just telling you. You truly are on an adventure. Do you know how many have made it this far? None. But you did. They were too weak to press on."

"Or too wise," Alfonso countered. The Caretaker, however, did not take the remark lightly.

"Hey, I would show some respect if I were you. Towards me, towards our friend The Scribe," he said gesturing towards The Scribe, "and especially towards what you are about to encounter behind that door," he concluded with emphasis as he pointed towards the front door of the house. These last words, specifically, uneased Alfonso. He eyed the door with fearful curiosity.

"What about The Working Man?" he asked as he returned his focus to The Caretaker.

"Don't get me started on The Working Man," The Caretaker said in agitation.

"Okay-

"Calls himself The Working Man… That takes guts when you stand there in your fancy clothes, looking sharp, shouting for attention. Meanwhile, here I am having to rake the grass and the side pavement after I let you go. Those are the duties of a true working man. Let me ask you something, Alfonso. This might not appear to be a meaningful question, but it is. When you go to a café, what do you order?" Alfonso was taken aback by the question. *Truly out of left field*, he thought.

49

"Uhhh… Cappucino."

"Ahh… so you're one of them too."

"What do you order?" Alfonso asked after a slight pause, not knowing how to proceed.

"Straight black. And if I feel like it's going to be a good day, I will ask not to have the expired beans," he proudly said.

"I see," Alfonso said, dumbfounded. The Caretaker stood and smirked. A moment of silence was shared between the two. And as always, the faint sound of writing remained.

"You're probably wondering why the hell we've been having this conversation."

"That is a fair assumption."

"Alfonso," The Caretaker began, "Every journey, every quest, every story, every adventure, has a small collection of required events and personnel. Are you following me?" Alfonso nodded. "Good. You are the protagonist of this story. Our mutual friend The Scribe is its orator. Our not so mutual friend, The Working Man, is its spark. And I am the obstacle."

"You're the obstacle? Not what lies behind that door?"

"I'll admit that what you will encounter behind that door is terrifying, disturbing, and, as some would boldly say, incomprehensibly grotesque. But no, not the obstacle."

"Okay," Alfonso said with concern, "Then what exactly do I have to overcome?"

"As of now, nothing."

"Nothing?"

"Nothing. You have already overcome your obstacle." Alfonso maintained his dumbfounded expression, and not by choice. He was truly lost in the convoluted games played by The Caretaker, and presumably The Scribe and The Working Man. "What did I overcome?" he asked.

"Me."

"But what did I do?"

"You listened."

"That's it?"

"Yes," The Caretaker said, laughing. "As silly as this may sound, it is the truth. You listening and putting up with my antics speaks volumes. We live in a world where interjections, interruptions, and volume symbolize strength. But if no one ever listens, how will we identify the good and the bad? How will we ever learn to compromise? To understand one another. A yappy, self-righteous, attention-seeking clown like The Working Man, would have tried talking over and outsmarting me. I would have hated it, then he also would have eventually hated it and left. You stayed, listened, humbly held your ground, and still continue to

51

pursue the ends of this simple task. Even with all these lunacies you have met and experienced! I call that something to be proud of."

"He's right, you know," The Scribe chimed in, Alfonso surprised, "I was hoping for more action after seeing you get antsy earlier, but you just had to ruin it for me, didn't you?" he teased.

"Hey!" The Caretaker shouted, "I'm supposed to be the cruel one. I dish out the fear and abuse. You're already telling the damn story! Know your role and play within it. You see?! Another example on how they stomp on the true working man."

"Stop trying to romanticize your reality," The Scribe fired back, but not as aggressively, "I have kept my mouth shut this whole time to let you have your moment. Your life is not that difficult."

"Are you listening, Alfonso? This is the kind of classist abuse I have taken, and continue to take in this role. They don't understand what I have gone through. This used to be my home. And then one day, it no longer was…"

"You willingly sold it!"

"Lies! I was coerced by what lives beyond that door," he said eerily. "But such is life, Alfonso. This is where my spiel comes to an end. I am grateful to have met you, and wish you the best of luck." The Caretaker then walked towards the side of the house until he vanished. Alfonso remained at the gate, with mixed emotions. There was something oddly comforting about The Caretaker's presence. A certain honesty that settled Alfonso's thoughts. Or maybe it was just his striking outfit, something Alfonso had never seen. And probably for the better. Whatever this presence was, life was noticeably different without it. And the idea of meeting what lay 'beyond that door' became that much more daunting.

"He's right," The Scribe said.

"About?"

"Wishing you the best of luck. You'll need it."

5 – Beyond the Door

The Scribe's comments were of no help or comfort to Alfonso, and Alfonso expected nothing less from his apparent side. He wondered if The Scribe made such comments to spice up the narrative he was constructing. Or whether he wished to emphasize the scale of this journey to motivate Alfonso. Whatever the reasons, they improved nothing from Alfonso's perspective. He remained uneasy but curious, as he eyed the door from where he stood behind the gate. *This was it*, he thought. This was the end, the final destination of the 'simple task' he had agreed to complete. Supposedly. He had in fact taken The Caretaker's lesson to heart.

And so it began. Cautiously, Alfonso once again reached over to unlock the gate. He flicked the latch loose and let the gate open on its own. The gate opened slowly, making a slight creak as it welcomed our dear Alfonso, but our friend remained still. He analyzed the entirety of the house's front yard and entrance, his eyes panning from left to right. Nothing. No one. Not a leaf in flight. Not a caretaker in sight. Rather, an Alfonso in fright. Alfonso still found it unnerving that not one person had walked by this entire time, but such was the reality of this 'simple task'. He commenced his march to the door.

Step by step, he made his way across the concrete path and up the few stairs that would complete his ascent to the entrance of the home. His advance proved to be uneasy. A gentle wind whistled its way through the front yard, shaking the bushes and jittering Alfonso. A crow then joined, loudly cawing and flying circles over our protagonist's crossing. *Not exactly the best of omens… Impeccable timing.* He did his best to block the haunting sounds as he made his final steps towards the door.

The door itself was grandiose in appearance, but not necessarily in size. It was wooden with a light stain, contained the traditional carvings that gave it its grand old feel, and hosted a black metal knocker about halfway up from its center. Alfonso scanned the entrance way. It was empty. He looked back to The Scribe. His company had yet to move, standing in the exact same spot, this time smiling and waving. *How comforting.* Alfonso turned his attention back to the door. He reached for the knocker, pulled it back, and prepared to release it. He held on a few moments more, calming his breathing. *This is it. You made it. You should be proud. All you have to do is release the instrument in your hand, greet the resident of this home, deliver the case, and you will have fulfilled this quest. This 'simple task'. All is well.* A baby smile was born. Alfonso took one final breath, calmly exhaled, and released the knocker.

It was one of those moments where life stood still. The moment Alfonso let go, everything came to a halt. He watched on, holding his breath. The Scribe stood ready to ready to write, anxiously awaiting the next chapter of his tale. Some even say that The Caretaker was peering from around the corner, eagerly hoping for Alfonso to be the first to succeed. That, I cannot confirm, but feel should be mentioned. Nevertheless, there was significant weight to knocker, of both the symbolic and physical variety, as it flew to alert its host.

Bang! The door flew open, startling Alfonso. He finally saw what The Caretaker had been alluding to. Standing in the doorway was a man of stocky build. He had pale skin and thick brown hair. Like The Caretaker, the man's choice of attire proved difficult to ignore. He wore a short-sleeved Hawaiian button up, a pair of dark baggy dress pants, brown leather slippers, and sported a pair of cheap sunglasses you would find at the local dollar store. In addition to his dazzling attire, he was breathing extremely heavily – on the brink of panting. Nevertheless, he maintained a fixed composure on Alfonso, who remained still. The visual was yet another perplexing one, but it was coupled with what appeared to not be a choice in presentation. As he initially scanned the man, he looked twice when he saw, what appeared to be, blood on the knuckles of the man's right hand. *Now that is a legitimate concern,* Alfonso anxiously thought. *Stand still and wait for him to speak.* "Are you Alfonso?" the man asked, his voice low and raspy. *And he knows my name.*

"Yes."

"Do you have the- the case?" he asked, struggling to articulate his question.

"Yes," Alfonso said showing him the case.

"Give it to me." Alfonso handed him the case. The man accepted. He took a long look at it, and then Alfonso. "Wait here." He darted inside, shutting the door in a flash. Silence. Alfonso turned to face The Scribe. He was not writing on this one occasion. In fact, he shrugged as if to say he was puzzled by the man's actions. Alfonso's expression was also one of confusion, though his inner thoughts knew better. *Business as usual.* But suddenly, there came a loud smash. Alfonso spun around. It sounded as if something glass-made and fragile had met its end. The door was closed. Silence. Alfonso stood still. He eyed the door with anticipation. The silence continued. *I hope he's okay...* He looked up to the knocker. *Wouldn't hurt.* He reached for it when a second smash erupted from inside. Alfonso froze. This time however, the noise was accompanied by violent shouting, "NOOOO! DEAR GOD, NOOOO!" Eyes wide open and mouth partially hanging, Alfonso remained anchored to the front steps. A couple more silent moments passed when the door abruptly flew open. The man returned,

57

briefcase in hand, violently panting, face visibly sweaty, and the blood on his knuckles that much fresher. Alfonso stood as still as a photograph. The man's breathing continued its volatile nature, gradually calming itself to what one may call 'heavy breathing'. It was in this state in which he handed Alfonso the case. Alfonso accepted the offering, carefully of course, not breaking eye contact. As soon as the case exchanged hands, the man spoke: "Return this case to The Working Man."

"Nicely done, my dear Alfonso!" The Working Man exclaimed in glee, his booming smile live and well, showcasing the case in his two hands.

"Should we be concerned with the man who wanted the case returned?" Alfonso rebutted in suspicion.

"You mean The Don?" The Working Man replied while fiddling with the case's clips. *The Don? Not a name I like to hear…*

"I guess so… yes. He never gave me his name."

"Nah nah, he's the last of your worries – a little rough around the edges, but harmless. Now, let's take a gander!" The Working Man opened the case, its contents facing him. Alfonso tried to peak and finally understand what he delivered there and back, but his initial reconnaissance failed. The Scribe, as always, stood behind our protagonist, completing his orthographic duties. Alfonso no longer wished, nor needed, to check on his company. He knew the drill. The Working Man began to chuckle, "Ha! I saw this coming." He then retrieved what was in the case, which Alfonso believed to be an envelope from its brief appearance, and added a replica. He closed the case and gave it back to Alfonso. "If you may, Alfonso, I will need you to take this back," he said happily. Alfonso took the case in surprise.

"I have to repeat what I just did?"

"Yes."

"And what would be the purpose in doing that?"

"Why, to fulfill the purpose of this simple task!"

"Which is..?"

"Yours to fulfill. And do not worry! You will be rewarded. Handsomely," The Working Man added with a grin. Alfonso replied with a blank stare. *Oh I'm sure I will.*

"Let's hope," he famously said. And off he went, back to the steps of The Don. The journey was not as memorable. Literally. The entire trek back to The Don's house, Alfonso did not make a sound; his mind fixated on what was in the case and how The Don would treat him this time around. Even the sounds of The Scribe's writing were muted.

Upon their arrival, Alfonso instantly noticed a difference. There was no Caretaker to be seen and the front gate was left open.

He paused to scan the front yard and entrance for a second time. Again, no one and nothing appeared. He continued to the door, The Scribe staying behind as he did before. Alfonso knocked. The door, yet again, flew open almost instantly. The man known as The Don presented himself in the exact same fashion using the exact same words, "Are you Alfonso?" *He can't be serious.*

"Yes…"

"Do you have the case?"

"Yes…"

"Give it to me." Alfonso handed him the case. "Wait here." The man ran inside, slamming the door. Alfonso then quickly turned to face The Scribe, who luckily was not writing.

"What's this all about?" he asked in a loud whisper. The Scribe delivered a sarcastic shrug. Alfonso sent expressions of disappointment and disapproval, when he was aggressively interrupted by abrupt screams and smashes from behind the door. It sounded as if plates were the choice this time, accompanied by intense screams voicing, "WHYYYYY?!" It took roughly ten to fifteen seconds for the commotion to settle, before the door swung open. The Don stood as he did earlier: sweaty, out of breath, somewhat bleeding, and offering the case back to our Alfonso.

"Return the case to The Working Man." These repeated words gave birth to a repeat of actions. Alfonso conducted this very same journey a total of six times that day.

"Typical," The Working Man said in laughter after viewing the contents of the case. Alfonso still could not see what was being placed inside, apart from his belief that it was sealed in an envelope. *Then what is the point of the case?* He wondered. Though, he quickly reminded himself that no question was really worth asking. He accepted his newly packed baggage and made his back to The Don.

The front gate was left open, again. *I guess communications are live and well.* The exchange was a complete replica. "Are you Alfonso?"

"Yes."

"Do you have the case?"

"Yes."

"Give it to me… Wait here," The Don dashing and the door shutting. The screams of desperation and disbelief were far more profound. "WHY MEEEE?!" The smashing also continued. *Glass again, I believe,* Alfonso thought. He had acclimatized to his new environment. The Don re-emerged in his frantic state, handed Alfonso the case, and uttered his usual request, "return the case to The Working Man."

"Amazing!" The Working Man exclaimed.

"FOR THE LOVE OF GOD, NOOOOO!"

"Spectacular!"

"PLEASE! PLEASE! PLEASE... NOOOOO!" and the shattering of fragile objects ensued. Alfonso stood patiently, waiting to complete the routine, and wondering how much more of his day it would take. He started in morning and was quickly catching late afternoon. *This has certainly been an... interesting day.* The door swung open. The Don was as he had been all day. *Okay, lay it me on. 'Return the case to The Working Man',* Alfonso mocked mentally. "Tell The Working Man that I want his head," The Don stated. Alfonso did not freeze, as he had not been moving, but his eyes widened. *His head? THE DON wants a head...* He did not know what to say. "Did you hear me?" The Don asked in a borderline threatening manner.

"Yes," Alfonso quietly mustered.

"Good," replied The Don, tossing the case to Alfonso's feet, "because if things don't go as planned, you will find yourself in an unfortunate... situation."

"Outstanding!" The Working Man announced in glee. Alfonso watched on as his employer joyfully made his way through the case. Alfonso was not one to be a bearer of bad news, but felt that interrupting The Working Man's fun was an absolute necessity.

"He also said that he wanted your head," Alfonso said quickly and unexpectedly. The Working Man paused his business and looked up towards Alfonso, his face partially confused, but soon home to his addictive smile.

"Did he now? That man is a clown. Well, let's see how he finds things this time," he cheerfully concluded by closing the case and enthusiastically throwing into Alfonso's arms. Alfonso received and cradled the case with anxious curiosity. *I still don't know what's inside,* he thought as he listened to The Scribe's writing, reminding him of everything he had gone through to reach this point. *My life was threatened. I must know.*

"What's in it?" he bluntly asked. The Working Man let out his customary laugh.

"We've been through this my dear Alfonso. You must never know."

"I respectfully disagree," Alfonso boldly stated, "he threatened my life. I have to know." The Working Man maintained his typically joyful expressions, but it was clear that hints of concern were breaking through. He did not expect Alfonso to push back in such a manner.

"What did I say earlier?" he began, "The man is a clown. There is nothing to be concerned about."

"Easy to say, not so easy to believe," Alfonso fired back. "The man has blood on his knuckles, he passionately smashes anything fragile he can get his hands on, he screams in desperation and anger, and threatens both you and me."

"A true character," The Working Man said, "rare to meet, but fun to greet." But Alfonso was not having any of these fun and games. He started opening the case. "Wait, what are you doing?" The Working Man asked, this time in grave concern. His notorious smile vanished. Alfonso ignored his words and continued on. "Alfonso, you shouldn't take him seriously. He's a strange person, but believe me, there is nothing to be afraid of." Alfonso again ignored him. "Please! Don't!" The Working Man shouted in fear, but it was too late. Alfonso opened the case, retrieved the envelope he had correctly observed, and ripped it open. Inside, was a small slip of paper neatly folded in four. *This is it. This is what I have risked my life for.* He unfolded the slip. Silence. The Working Man stood in agony, pale as a pearl. The Scribe had paused his scripture to observe Alfonso's next move. Alfonso took his time absorbing the contents of the slip. He lowered his findings to face The Working Man.

"Bishop to F4?" The Scribe rushed back to his duties. The Working Man did not speak. "You're playing chess, and I'm your messenger?" Alfonso asked in agitation.

"There is more to it than just that!" The Working Man replied in desperation. A silence ensued. Alfonso shook in disbelief. *All this… All this… for what? To be played.* He faced The Working Man once more, showcasing his immense disappointment. The Working Man continued to stand in fear, but cracked a smile as he faced Alfonso. "Allow me to explain," he said. At the sound of those words, Alfonso dropped the case and its contents, and departed the hidden center of the park. "Alfonso, no! Alfonso!" The Working Man cried. Alfonso ignored his pleas. He did not even look at The Scribe. "He was the best we ever had," The Working man stated, "Let's hope he understands."

"Prayed The Working Man," added The Scribe with his cheeky grin, before watching Alfonso's figure disappear into the trees.

6 – The Following Year

One year had passed since that fateful day. Alfonso had restored his daily rituals. The city gardens were once again his second home, the willow his friend, and his notebook the keeper of his thoughts. No contact between himself and the fellows he met on that fateful day had been made. Life was good for our dear protagonist. He lay under his friend the willow and reminisced on the events of a year ago.

I feel fortunate to tell you, my humble listener, that what you are about to read are Alfonso's exact words, recorded in his notebook, from this exact day. Do not ask how I came about such information. That will be revealed in due time. Hopefully. For now, let us join our friend on this beautiful June day.

Today marks the one-year anniversary of that unfortunate day. The day I tried to alter my life, and ended up used by a collection of... weirdos. I honestly cannot think of a better word, so allow me to apologize to whomever reads this. What a bizarre group of people... You always hear of the strange personalities that exist out there, but you never truly accept their existence until you actually witness it. I finally witnessed it a year ago and am thankful to be free from them now. Not to sound too dramatic, but my life has been restored. I'm back baby. My solitude is back. This beautiful garden is back. The people who appreciate it alongside me are back. And no, I do not refer to my friend the willow, though he is just as happy, but rather a new friend. Kenneth! We bonded over our love of the gardens not too long ago. I'll admit, it took me a while to accept his form of love, one more aesthetic than my own, but I have learned to be open and trust those around me. Kenneth has thanked me for being understanding. We now enjoy our company and co-admiration of the gardens on a weekly basis.

Unfortunately, that is all I have to offer. But do not fret! As our story continues…

Alfonso sat under the willow as he greeted Kenneth with a wave. Kenneth was above average in height while below average in build. He had long dark hair, a thick beard, and wore a green raincoat, dark pants, and boots. He acknowledged Alfonso's wave with a smile and a wave of his own, before withdrawing a pair of large garden clippers from underneath his coat. *The tools to capture his aesthetics. Hopefully, it's no more than two this week.* Alfonso closed eyes in fear of witnessing the brutality. He wished he had the courage to stand up to Kenneth, but *there is something so nice about him.* He froze for a few seconds, anticipating a snip, but rather heard chatter. He opened his eyes and found Kenneth talking to a stranger. A woman, to be specific. A beautiful woman. She had long brown hair, more on the darker end, and wore black-rimmed glasses, a dark sweater, jeans rolled up to just above her ankles, and a pair of worn sneakers. But what intrigued Alfonso more, was that she held a large book in her arms. It was a hardcover and had no visible title, as far as Alfonso could see. *What could she want?* Kenneth then pointed towards Alfonso. *Excuse me?* She spotted Alfonso, thanked Kenneth, and made her way over. Alfonso grew anxious as she approached. *What should I say? Hi? Hello?* "Hello!" the woman said enthusiastically, as she neared the willow. Alfonso just stared as she came to a stop, simply lost for words. She had piercing green eyes and a quaint necklace of a sailboat.

"Hello," Alfonso finally said.

"Are you Alfonso?" she asked.

"Yes… Who is asking?"

"I would tell you my name, but after reading this I feel like that wouldn't be so exciting." Alfonso eyed the book.

"Okay then… what is that exactly?"

"A gift for you!"

"From whom?" Alfonso asked suspiciously.

"From a mutual friend. They said that's all I could tell you, and that you would understand once you read it. So here you go." She gave the book to Alfonso, who accepted it with curiosity.

"How did you find me?"

"I was told to enjoy a day at the gardens, maybe find some inspiration for my own work, and look for someone named Alfonso, who would most likely be relaxing and/or writing under a tree or around the flowers!" Alfonso went silent for a few moments.

"And you can't tell me who it's from?" he asked while examining the book.

"They said you would understand when you read it."

"I'm not sure I want to read it."

"What? Why?" she responded in shock.

"It's a long a story, but what I will say is that you could only understand if you were here a year earlier. This all seems... To not be a coincidence of timing, and it's quite unnerving."

"Strange... That's not how you were described."

"I'm almost positive you weren't told everything."

"No no. In the book." Alfonso froze. His eyes lit up in surprise. "Oops!" she said sarcastically.

"We both know the person who gave it to you," he quietly muttered to himself. "Who are you?"

"Like I said, I can't give you my name. However, people know me as The Stranger. Or L'etranger, if you prefer. I am an artist. I also work at a local café – The Blanc Mug. It's a great spot for all artists, old and new. That is how I met our mutual friend. You should pop by sometime. Maybe you'll spot them." And with that, The Stranger left Alfonso with a smile.

"Wait! You can't just leave me hanging like this," Alfonso called out. The Stranger stopped and turned to speak one last time.

"Read the book! I want to hear your thoughts." And she vanished into the gardens. Alfonso stared off in frustration, before turning his attention to his gift.

"Promise you won't haunt me," he demanded of his gift. He paused, took a deep breath, exhaled, and opened the book. His eyes widened and his heart began to race. "Happy anniversary," he said to himself as he read the following title:

Heroic Tales of the Present – Book I: The Tale of Alfonso, A Life Worth Living

Manufactured by Amazon.ca
Bolton, ON

13533597R10042